Dirrarn

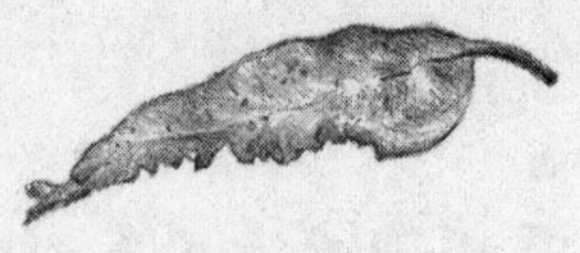

We acknowledge and pay respects to the Noongar and Jaru Elders past, present and future – the traditional custodians of the lands on which this book is set.

This book was made possible by the Daisy Utemorrah Award. We acknowledge and commemorate her contribution to the sharing of knowledge and wisdom through story.

We are so thankful to Rachel Bin Salleh, Sharona Wilson and the Magabala Books team for believing in us and Mia's story. It has been a wonderful journey working with you all.

We give thanks to our writing mentor, Shel Sweeney, from A Worded Life, and our agent, Alex Adsett. Thanks to the Kimberley Language Resource Centre for their support with our language.

This book is dedicated to all the remote First Nations children who dream big at home or away.

Your future isn't gifted to you from any teacher or school, you hold the power to shape your future in your hands.

Dream big and fly high.

This is a Magabala Book

Leading Publisher of Aboriginal and
Torres Strait Islander Storytellers.

Changing the World, One Story at a Time.

First published 2023. Reprinted 2024 x2, 2025 x2
Magabala Books Aboriginal Corporation
1 Bagot Street, Broome, Western Australia
Website: www.magabala.com Email: sales@magabala.com

Magabala Books is assisted by the Australian Government through Creative Australia, its principal arts investment and advisory body. The State of Western Australia has made an investment in this project through the Department of Local Government, Sport and Cultural Industries.

Magabala Books is Australia's leading independent Aboriginal and Torres Strait Islander publishing house. Magabala Books acknowledges the Traditional Owners of the Country on which we live and work. We recognise the unbroken connection to traditional lands, waters and cultures. Through what we publish, we honour all our Elders, peoples and stories, past, present and future.

Carl Merrison & Hakea Hustler are the recipients of the Daisy Utemorrah Award. Presented within the WA Premier's Book Awards, the Daisy Utemorrah Award recognises excellence in junior and YA fiction and seeks to grow Indigenous writing for younger readers. Magabala Books acknowledges the Copyright Agency Cultural Fund and the State Government of Western Australia for their support of the Daisy Utemorrah Award.

Cover by Jo Hunt
Typeset by Post Pre-press Group
Printed by Griffin Press

A catalogue record for this book is available from the National Library of Australia

• 978-1-922777-02-7 (Print) • 978-1-922777-00-3 (ePDF) •
978-1-922777-01-0 (ePUB)

Dirrarn

Carl Merrison
& Hakea Hustler

Illustrated by Dub Leffler

1

The hit came hard, sending Naya reeling from her spot on the playground bench.

Charlotte jogged over to collect her ball, Naya lay sprawled on the ground stunned.

'Don't you have something to say?' Mia said, hands on hips, staring Charlotte down.

'I do,' Charlotte whirled around. 'I'll say "Get lost, Mia!"'

Mia bent down and scooped up Naya, put her arm around her friend. 'Whatever, Charlotte. Learn to kick before you run your mouth.'

Charlotte's cheeks burned red and she scoffed, 'Like you'd know anything, bush pig. Learn to talk properly before you run *your* mouth.'

With anger boiling and frustrated tears in her eyes, Mia felt like lunging at Charlotte and wiping the smug look off her face. Naya swayed, and Mia held her tighter and turned to guide her away. Charlotte was talking about Mia's accent, a result of being a Jaru and Aboriginal English speaker, with Standard Australian English her third language. Mia had never really realised she spoke differently than anyone else until she came to Perth.

Mia felt helpless in this place. Back home, in her school, she knew how to deal with things like that. Here, at this fancy boarding school, they had different rules, different ways of dealing with bullies like Charlotte. Mia never felt like it was actually dealt with. Charlotte's behaviour just then was proof of that.

Mia walked Naya around the corner towards the office, unsure what type of help her new friend needed.

'We don't be unkind just for the fun of it, Charlotte,' Ms Greenhalge said sternly, walking swiftly over after catching the last of the altercation, her position of authority as a teacher stopped Charlotte mid-jog.

'It was just an accident, Ms Greenhalge,' Charlotte replied sweetly, eyes looking up innocently at the teacher with a sweet smile. 'We were just having fun.'

Ms Greenhalge picked up the ball at Charlotte's feet.

'If you can't kick properly or speak with kindness, you'll have to lose this one then,' the teacher said sternly. 'You'll make your peace with Naya and Mia before you get it back. You can follow me now.'

Charlotte didn't argue but when Ms Greenhalge turned to walk away, Charlotte stuck out her tongue and mimed the teacher's words quietly before following.

On the other side of the school, Mia and Naya sat under a large old gumtree. Gaalyalya chattered and squawked in the branches above. Mia was aware that they carried a different name on Noongar Country.

'I'm proper wild at that Charlotte, bi,' Naya said once the dull ache in her back and head had subsided. She had refused to go to the school sickbay, preferring the comfort of her new friend than the strange new office staff. Naya had come from a community 'down the road' from Mia but they were still separated by distance and hours. The girls had never met before they both started term a few weeks ago. It turned out they had other connections.

'True,' Mia replied, tightening her fists at the memory. 'Proper stuck up, high class, thinks she is untouchable.'

'Well, she is not,' Naya said. 'One day she'll get what's coming.'

'It makes me slack them teachers taking sides,' Mia pulled out a snack from her bag, oblivious to Ms Greenhalge's actions. 'They never deal with it properly here. Charlotte and her gang get away with everything.'

Mia felt so far from home. Growing up in a remote outback community, she had still faced her fair share of bullies. She'd dealt with it in her own way then. Telling a teacher sometimes worked, other times a big brother or sister or family put a stop to it. Everyone back home knew how things worked. Here it was just her and Naya. Mia had pushed Charlotte away the first time and had been met with larger reprimands than Charlotte. Mia didn't feel seen or heard by the teachers. They did things differently here.

Mia's hand unconsciously went to her

birthmark between her shoulder blades. It reminded her of her strength and connection. Maybe she was only strong on her Country.

She remembered a story her grandmother had told her. An old story passed down from Elder to community for generations since Creation. This story spoke of responsibility and consequence. But here on Noongar Country she felt far away from her ancestors, far away from her people. And this school was ruled by teachers of different heritages, too. Mia wondered if the story and its message reached here.

It was only first term and Mia was sick. Homesick. Sick of this place. Sick of the rules. Sick of the way she and Naya had been treated. She wanted to go home.

2

The chorus of voices hummed as Mia walked into the dining hall with the twelve other boarders. Mr Cale, a boarding house carer, jostled around the tables filling the trays with dinner food.

As the students found their places, Ms Babel, the other boarding house carer, sat down on a shared dining table with them. Mia and Naya sat at the end of the table, sitting quiet ways. In both girls' cultures, you didn't always have to fill the silence with small talk or chatter. They didn't have much to talk about and were still feeling down after their interaction with Charlotte at lunchtime.

Ms Babel noticed the way the girls' shoulders slumped and the flat expressions on their faces. She was used to giving pastoral care to girls from remote communities. She'd worked as a 'house parent' for many years and had seen countless students from remote outback towns come and go. She knew the difference between the body language.

'What's up, Mia and Naya?' Ms Babel asked in a soft voice, resting her hand gently on the back of Mia's chair.

Mia and Naya looked at each other without moving their heads, a flick of the eyes. Ms Babel had been kind to them and helped them feel settled in their new boarding home. She had sat with Naya when she had been sick a few weeks ago. She had helped Mia figure out the school timetable. After their bad experience with teachers dealing with Charlotte and her group at school, they weren't sure what to tell Ms Babel. Would it just end up being worse for them again?

Mia flicked her hand, sign language everyone used back home to mean 'nothing'.

'We right, Miss,' Naya replied, looking up at Ms Babel. 'Just hungry for this feed.'

'You know you can always talk to me, don't you?' Ms Babel raised an eyebrow.

The two girls nodded and Ms Babel sat with them a little longer, allowing the silence to stretch. Soon she stood up to join Mr Cale with the food.

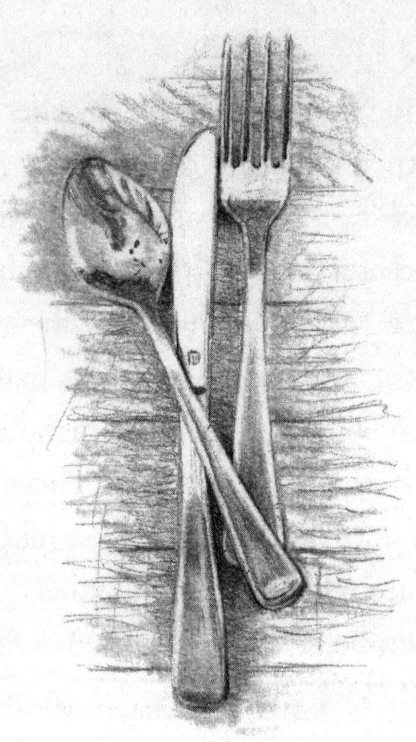

‘What you reckon?’ Mia said, when Ms Babel was busy. ‘Should we have told her about Charlotte today?’

‘Nah,’ Naya replied. ‘We’d probably end up getting trouble about it somehow, too.’

‘I don’t get how she gets away with it, true God,’ Mia replied. ‘Teacher’s pet? Her family rich or something?’

'Most that mob are rich enough I reckon. Think the school fees here are thousands,' Naya said, picking up her plate now that Ms Babel had called students over to serve themselves from the hot trays at the front table. The smell of roast chicken, seasoned vegetables and gravy wafted across the room. 'It feels like they do everything different here, hey? Classes, homework, extracurricular clubs, uncomfortable uniforms.'

'My aunty told me about this thing called "culture shock" where you get slack and sick from all the different ways of doing things in that other place,' Mia said to her new friend. 'It is so different here.'

'Well, I'm Charlotte sick. I'll have to decide if I've got that culture sick later,' Naya laughed.

The other students on the table came from different places all over the state, too. A few students from the Pilbara, a few from the Wheatbelt, and Naya and Mia from the Kimberley. Life at the hostel wasn't too much different than home. Both girls were used to living in houses full of people, the hustle and bustle in the kitchen. The other students talked Aboriginal English with them even if everyone didn't share the same traditional languages and slang. The mob in here 'got them'.

The bedtimes were strict, and it was strange not having family in and out visiting and coming to yarn up around a fire. The fancy school was heaps different from home, and Mia wondered if it would get easier. It had already been six weeks.

Soon all the boarders were getting up to serve themselves from the selection of food and settling down to eat. Mia and Naya let the troubles of the day wash away with mouthfuls of roast vegetables and sips of orange juice.

3

In the morning, Mia looked around for her schoolbooks. Turns out they were right where she had left them, forgotten – under her school shirt by her jaja's dirrarn painting on her chest of drawers. Tiredly, she remembered how she was meant to have done some homework for a class today. Homework was a bit new to her. She'd seen it in schools in movies, and had to do the occasional home task back in her small community school, but here they gave something almost every day.

The threat of having to stay in over lunch in 'homework class' like the first time she had missed her homework was enough to have Mia sneaking over to Tilly's room early. A Year 11 student from the Pilbara who had been schooling away here for years, Tilly was a good type – friendly with a deadly sense of humour who knew a little of Mia's Country. She had relatives from a community near Mia's. They had been paired up as boarding buddies in case Mia ever needed help.

Mia tapped lightly on the door, 'You awake, Til?'

Back home, with a blood relative, Mia might have bounced into a cousin-sister's room and jumped on the bed to wake them up. But here, every girl had their own private room and Mia wasn't that close to Tilly or even Naya yet. Tilly opened her door, hair messy and eyes bleary.

'What na, Mia-girl?' Tilly asked, opening her door wider to let Mia in then crawling back into her bed.

'I'm bin forget that stupid homework from yesterday, bi,' Mia said, perching on the end of Tilly's bed. 'Any chance you can help me out real quick?'

'Really?' Tilly grumbled, pulling the sheets over her head. 'You had Babel and Cale bugging mob last night for homework. Why didn't you do it then?'

'I was distracted. Had a bad day at school, you know? Just needed to chill out last night and … I forgot,' Mia said. 'Not used to this homework stuff here yet.'

'Get it out then,' Tilly said finally, swinging her legs back out to sit next to Mia on the bed. 'What got you all wild at school, huh?'

As Mia went through her books and scrambled pieces of paper looking for the homework sheet, she told Tilly the story about Charlotte yesterday and, really, all term. She blurted out her frustrations with the different ways of doing things here and how she felt like Charlotte and her friends got away with their nasty behaviour. The judgey looks, the comments under their breath, the feet that popped out from under desks as she passed. All subtle, discreet, hard to prove. The labels of 'bush pig', 'poor girl' and 'Centrelink handout'.

Tilly was a good listener. Mia had found the homework sheet in the middle of her story and handed it to Tilly.

'Okay, problem one,' Tilly said after Mia had finished. 'You gotta be smarter than that

Charlotte girl. She is trying to pull you into trouble her way. She knows how these teachers work and how this school works. You don't know the rules and the culture here yet. She trapping you like a fly in a spider web. Don't play her games. You avoid her and ignore her and you do you. You aren't here for that stuck-up chick. You here for you and your mob. You gotta be smarter and stronger. You just wait till you understand the game and you'll find your way to put her back in her place. This world is full of Charlottes.'

Tilly sounded like a proper old woman to Mia, with all her advice. It sounded like something her jawiji would say if she had told him about it. It was true, too. Charlotte knew how to bait Naya and Mia, and so far they had fallen for it each time. Mia was going to be like the galbun, circling and watching from further away, watching and learning. She wasn't going to be the bug in Charlotte's web.

'And problem number two,' Tilly said, turning her attention to the worksheet in her hands. 'They said it in a long confusing way but basically this task is asking you to write about something important to you. Just write about something back home you love.'

'Thanks, Tilly,' Mia said sincerely. 'Don't know how you figured all this stuff out down here. Do you ever miss home?'

'I miss home all the time,' Tilly replied. 'You just got to learn to code-switch and be strong both ways. I'll be back home bigger and better each holidays anyway, and only two more years of school for me. I'm almost done, then I'll be on Country for as long as I want.'

With only an hour until the boarders would be called down for breakfast, Mia quickly began work on her homework task. Right now she missed and loved everything about home. She missed the deep, cool waterholes. She missed the open plains and hunting jarrambayi. She missed painting with her jaja and aunties. She loved them all. She even missed her brother, Jy, who hadn't returned from Law before she had gotten on the plane to boarding school.

But as Mia put pen to paper, instead she found herself writing about something else. Not too many months before, she had had to make the difficult choice to let go an injured dirrarn that she had been caring for. Her jarriny was a wild black cockatoo, had been miserable in its cage in Mia's backyard. She had known she would have to set it free.

Boarding school had been Mia's chance to soar far from home. At the moment, she didn't like where she had landed.

By the time the call for breakfast came, Mia had finished writing.

4

The clean, even footpath led the way from the boarding house to Mia's new school, a five-minute walk. Naya walked to Mia's left, filling her in on some of the drama from back home that she had found out about on the phone with one of her cousins the night before. A cool wind swept up grass clippings and leaves from the garden beds and pushed it lazily onto the path. A flock of gaalyalya squawked and played in the shade of a large old gumtree. They kind of looked odd in the city. Their squawks were drowned out by the busy traffic noise.

A P-plater, wearing the local public school uniform, beeped his horn and hollered as he drove by, startling the two girls. This road was busy enough and they didn't know the people around here. That senior boy could have been yelling teasing way or worse. Mia and Naya knew that boys yelling things out of cars could be dangerous. They'd heard the stories of bad things. Both girls would consider themselves tough and smart, able to hold their own back home. They'd learnt to hunt, shoot, and spear fish and even how to fight if they had to. But an older man, with or without a car as a weapon, far away from home still made the girls nervous.

'What kind?' Naya said angrily, sticking her finger up at the retreating car. 'Think'm self, shouting out to us for nothing.'

'Think they own the street I reckon. Or just teasing us for this private school uniform?' Mia replied, copying Naya's actions at the car. The girls had heard there was some rivalry between the public school and private one. Mia kind of understood it, too. The private school students didn't mind flouting the best brands and tech.

Mia was relieved when they passed through the school gates. It was still surreal passing through different school gates for the past month and a half. For every other school day of her life she'd passed through her metal wire school gates and been surrounded by her cousin-sisters and friends. They'd kick around on the oval, barefoot and laughing, sweat dripping in the early morning heat.

Here she passed through heavy stone walls and intricate iron gates and was surrounded by cookie-cutter strangers in neatly ironed blue school uniforms. Mia and Naya walked to the room of their first class and sat down on the bench outside watching the other students file by.

Her school at home and this one were steeped in 100 years of history. These histories made Mia feel sad and uncomfortable.

'What do you reckon the kids back home would be doing right now at your school?' Mia asked Naya, leaning back against the wall and staring up at the clouds.

'I'd be getting on the school bus with my sisters from out la block,' Naya said. 'Then we'd get a feed at breakfast club and shoot around basketball till the bell went.'

And right then, as if on cue, the bell went.

'My aunty who works at the school would probably be plaiting my hair. Then I'd help my little cousins to class,' Mia said as they both found their spot in line.

Family was everything and everywhere back in the Kimberley. Here, Mia looked around the line of blue and white, and felt like she was the odd one out.

5

Tilly's advice to stay away from Charlotte and her friends was easier said than done. They were timetabled into Science, Mathematics and Computer classes together. Mia made sure to circle around the outside of the room in the opposite direction of Charlotte, watching her like a galbun. She found a seat in the middle row and Naya sat down beside her. Ms Layland began her lesson on rock types. It made Mia think of the layered mountains back home and where they had been pushed out of the earth at jutting angles. It reminded her of the cliffs where her cousin, Scotty, had found an ancient spearhead that he had been given permission to gift to her. That artifact was under her pillow back at the hostel, for her to smooth her hands over before sleep and link her to home and history.

Soon they were at their metal experiment tables smashing conglomerate rocks to see what they were made of. The piece that Naya and Mia had been given was full of small, trapped shells. They had to hypothesise what it was made of, where it had been formed and where it had been found. Right here, in this fancy old school, Mia could empathise with those trapped shells.

Mia knew in theory she should be grateful for this opportunity. Many of the kids from her community and others in the Kimberley would never be given the chance to school away. Maybe they had too much of a bad school record, or they weren't literate enough, or their families weren't able to fill out the right forms at the right time. Some communities had small high school classes and some didn't have high schools at all. School was meant to be universal and free access for all kids in Australia. But it didn't really feel that way. And standing there, in a state-of-the-art science lab, Mia wondered if it was really that equitable at all.

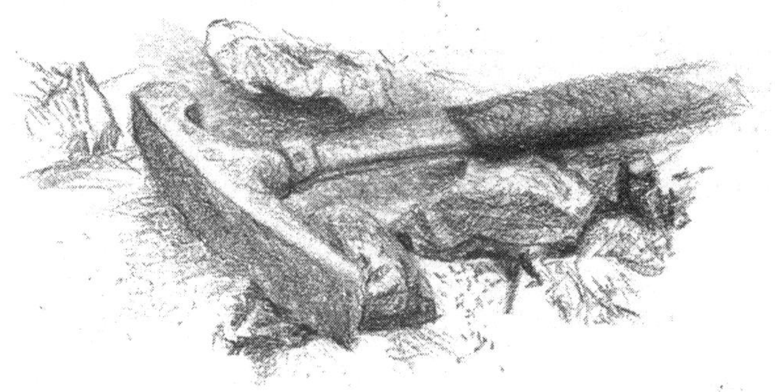

Mia had felt so nervous and excited and a weight of responsibility on her shoulders when she had been given her spot at the school. A chance to make her family proud. See places she'd only seen on television. Skyrises, shopping centres, movie cinemas.

'I think it's baby river shells pressed down by mud and silt,' Naya hypothesised. 'From the Swan River. Digging up the Noongar mob's old middens.'

'I think it's probably old ocean layers. Like they have out Fitzroy Crossing way on Bunuba Country. That area used to be ocean they reckon.'

They wrote their answers down on a whiteboard and put it in front of their crushed rock. The teacher had them walk around checking out all the other rock types from each group and their written hypothesis.

'I didn't know we were letting wild bush chickens into exclusive private schools,' Charlotte said at the perfect volume to be just heard by Mia, and just not heard by Ms Layland. 'Look at this chicken-scratch handwriting. Guess they didn't teach writing in the outback chook schools.'

Mia wanted to peck Charlotte's eyes –

chicken-style, if that's what Charlotte wanted. It took all Mia's self-control to remember to be the galbun. Circling, aloof, not getting involved in the spider's trap.

Naya made to move forward, but Mia had to hold her back. 'Leave her.'

Charlotte's friends burst out laughing and moved onto the next table.

Finally back at their table, Naya took the small rock hammer and pounded their crushed rock again.

6

Mia was happy the weekend arrived. Ms Babel had arranged a visit to the Perth Zoo for the boarders who wanted to go and Mr Cale was staying behind with anyone who needed to stay home for the weekend. That included those who had big assignments, those who were grounded or some who had family coming to check them out for the weekend.

Naya and Mia opted for the zoo. Mia had enjoyed the four outings with the boarding school mob so far and had only missed one when she had been late on an English assignment. She'd been to the local pool, the beach twice, and a skate park. Each time Mia's knowledge of and appreciation for the city grew. It was like she was putting together a jigsaw puzzle of the city in her head. She was proud of each new piece she placed.

Mia was pretty sure the zoo was larger than her whole community back home and she hadn't even set foot inside yet.

Ms Babel gave the instructions on the main lawn – *go everywhere with a partner, keep phones on at all times, staff are available for help, meet back here around 11.30 for morning tea* – then the boarders were allowed to walk around with her and the group or go off in pairs.

Mia and Naya walked with Tilly and her friend Polly. They went past the African Savannah animals: the baboons, rhinoceroses, lions, giraffes, orangutans, elephants. Mia marvelled at the differences in looks, size, shape and skin of these animals that were so different to any she had seen. Of course, she had seen some of these in movies and documentaries, but it is one thing to see them on a screen and another to see them in person. Mia was amazed, but also a little sad. They were stuck so far from their homes in enclosures. And as nice, big and safe as the zoo was, it could never be the same as roaming large expanses with their families. She wondered if they had been born in captivity and known no different. Could you breed out the yearning for Country and family? Mia doubted it.

'Imagine these big fella roaming around back home,' Polly said, pointing to the large bull African elephant. 'Little scarier than coming across a booloomun in the scrub when mob out hunting.'

Tilly laughed, 'True, had a booloomun chase me too many times. They get into big trouble hunting endangered elephants, too. Like when hunting booloomuns.'

Despite being the traditional custodians of lands around each girl's home, First Nations peoples did not have free access to all areas. Booloomuns were property of the station owners – despite roaming freely over Country, off stations and on roads. Mia knew many Aboriginal mob had been massacred for hunting booloomuns and sheep in the early days.

'Don't think he would taste all that good anyway,' Polly joked, looking up at the giant creature. 'Think I'd rather marlu tail any day.'

'Don't be talking for bush tucker,' Naya pretended to whine. 'Make a girl hungry for home!'

Tilly pushed Naya's shoulder and ruffled

her hair, 'You don't get to adventure and hang with us girls back home, Naya-girl. Imagine all the stories you'll tell everyone back home, hey?'

Mia smiled as the older girls slung their arms around Naya's shoulders. Together they entered into a new exhibit: Asian Rainforest. The landscape became even more foreign with deep greens and lush plants. They looked at the gibbon, tiger and sun bears.

Polly used her phone to video call her family back home, who yarned excitedly as they saw the new animals through the phone.

'What you reckon, hungry Naya, you'd eat that one then?' Tilly teased, pointing to a large Komodo dragon. 'Maybe just a big jarrambayi or what?'

'Don't start, Tilly, or you'll have her packing for home when we get back to the hostel!' Mia laughed back as Naya pretended to hunt the large Asian lizard from their side of the glass.

Soon the girls stood at the sign for the Australian Bushwalk exhibits.

Polly's phone went off. 'It's time to meet back up at the main lawn you mob,' she said, switching off her alarm.

'Don't think that's such a bad thing,' Mia said to Polly. 'Think I might get too homesick or hungry heading into that one.'

'I hear you,' Polly replied. 'It gets a little easier, don't worry. School holidays coming up, you can be back in person soon!'

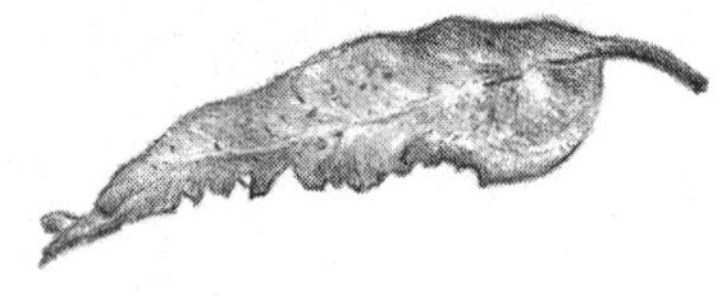

7

Mia sat eating her lunch with her friends under the pergola on the zoo's main lawn. The midday sun was warm and the gentle breeze provided soft relief. Mia watched Ms Babel yarning with the other students under a large old tree, the soft chatter reaching her ears intermingling with the sound of the zoo animals and, a little further and softer, the city sounds.

Mia was grateful to be sitting with her new friends. As hard as this whole term had been, she realised that she'd actually made some really good memories with this mob. Perhaps the strangeness, the newness, the discomfort was just her finding her wings.

For the time Mia had spent daydreaming about what was happening back at home, and the things she was missing out on, she had actually lost focus of the experiences she was having here.

Mia looked at the jiyirr birds, diving chasing insects, flying freely and landing in the tree above Ms Babel.

She remembered them from her Country, too. She wondered if these birds had travelled far from home like her. They looked plump, with slick feathers ready for a long flight. She wondered if they were heading home. Far away, like, and yet so unlike the animals locked in the zoo. She imagined the jiyirr as they travelled over green forests, speckled salt flats and red deserts. Had they spread their wings to travel over deep blue oceans to places far beyond the horizon too? Did they now chatter in the trees with stories of places they had seen, and other animals they had encountered?

Mia realised, as hard as it was, that she could take all these new experiences and bring back her stories. This could be a time that she would look back on and tell family about no matter where she ended up – either back home, staying in the city or on her next adventure. Mia was acutely aware that many people from her community had never left the Kimberley. She would never have to look at the remote teachers and nurses and police when they left town for Christmas and wonder what their place was like. She'd seen it now.

Ms Babel stood up and called them all over. The girls cleaned up their spot and walked over to join the others under a shady tree.

Ms Babel pointed out the map and the First Nations displays, and reminded everyone of expectations and the time to meet back up.

The zoo was getting busier now with families and tourists milling around. Mia and the other girls decided to go to the reptile enclosure before working their way up to the Australian animal exhibits. Inside the reptile exhibit, little children were tapping on the glass. As Mia stopped to look at the animal inside, a child looked up with curiosity at her, then ran over to his mother. He tugged at her shirt and pointed back at Mia. She bent down and pushed his hand back to his side and whispered to her child before shooting an embarrassed and apologetic smile back at Mia.

'Come on,' Naya said, encouraging the others further along to the Australian wetland exhibits. 'I gotta see my totem before we leave!'

'What one your totem animal then?' Polly said, pretending to look Naya up and down. 'You gotta be bilby – proper little and jumpy. Like on the basketball court.'

'Na, I reckon Naya is the dingo,' Tilly said playfully, slinging her arm over Naya's shoulder. 'All playful but licking her lips for that big lizard back there!'

Naya laughed and shrugged Tilly's arm off her shoulder. She picked up her pace as she walked towards the crocodile's enclosure. 'Close, Til, I'm the crocodile.'

'Remind me not to cross you then,' Polly

said, looking over the clear water of the exhibit at the large reptile laid out in the midday sun. 'You'll just lie in wait ready for payback.'

The water was clear, like some of the waterholes back home, but Mia knew crocodiles could be lurking in plain sight or deep in dirty waters. This made her think of Charlotte and the way she'd been avoiding her, learning the bully's game.

'You mob got jarriny too, or what?' Mia asked when they had moved on through the wetlands exhibit towards the Australian Bushwalk exhibit. Mia touched her hand to her back thinking of hers.

Polly and Tilly told the stories of their totems and how they had been given to them in their cultural ways as they passed the emus and the dingos.

'I have a whole necklace made from them porcupine spines at home,' Naya touched her

neck at the memory. 'My nanna made that one for me.'

Mia looked at the information plaque about the echidna. She liked that it had the Noongar name and information on there as well.

'It's strange, walking here with so many kangaroo,' Tilly said. 'Imagine if this marlu was like this back home!'

'Not sure there'd be much marlu back home,' Polly laughed.

'Look at this sign,' Naya pointed out the

sign that read 'Is there a roo with you?' on the gate of the next exhibit. 'These kangaroos would follow you home like takeaway!'

Mia could hear the squawks of her jarriny before she saw them. Her eyes had flicked to the sky in search of the passing dirrarn but then she realised the noise was from the bird just beyond the gate.

Mia was surprised to see information boards about cockatoo rescue and care, before her eyes fell on the large and multiple cages of rescued dirrarn. Turns out that farmers shot down the black cockatoo that lived on Noongar Country, they called them 'karrak' and that habitat destruction devastated their numbers. Mia's heart sank for the dirrarn that she had tried her best to rehabilitate and had ultimately decided to let go. The opportunities that her dirrarn might have had, had it been able to come to Perth, where they had the tools, equipment and funding to care for it. Mia was determined to learn more about how to care for injured animals and be the one to bring that knowledge back home to share. She wondered if one day the funding, tools and equipment might follow.

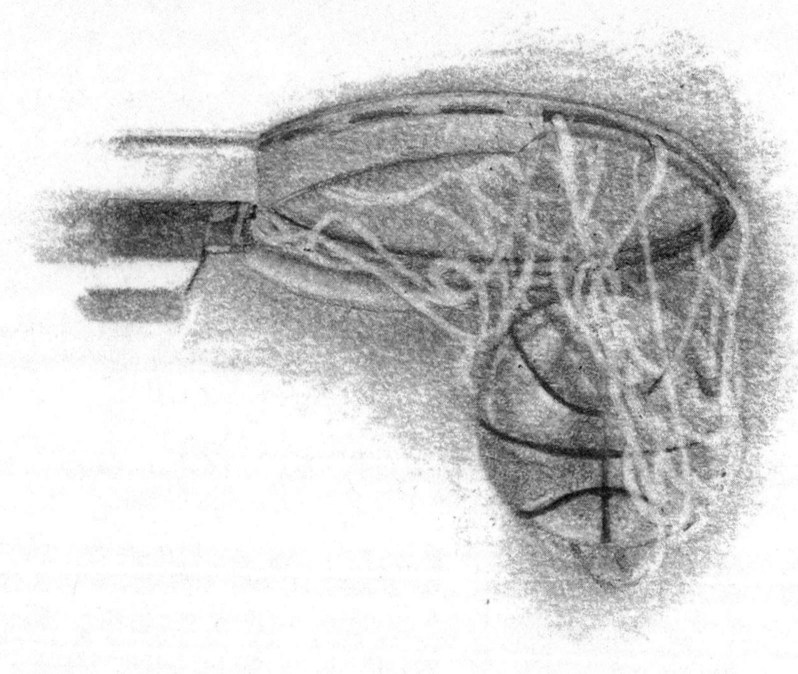

8

The weeks went by and Mia gained confidence at school. She still missed home, but she also looked forward to the new experiences and the new friendships she was forming every day. Mia and Naya now joined the older girls walking to school.

If they arrived at school early, before the buses arrived, they would shoot around on the basketball courts with some of the other early students. Mia liked showing off the moves she'd learned back home. She felt like they played a different version of basketball back there – raw and fast – compared to down here.

School breaks were spent kicking around on the oval, shooting hoops or hanging in the school quad with Naya, Tilly or Polly. Sometimes the other girls in Mia's class invited her to join them at the photography club or lunchtime art class.

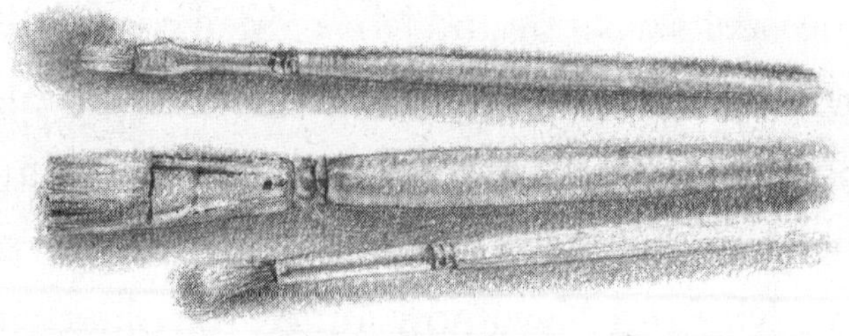

Charlotte and her gang still tried every opportunity to make Mia and Naya feel like outsiders who didn't belong. And Mia sometimes felt tempted to believe her. She didn't really see herself represented at school. Mia didn't see many faces like hers, hear accents like hers, see anything in the activities in classes that showed what her lived experience was. She didn't see the Aboriginal and Torres Strait Islander flags flying, or art by her people. She didn't see First Nations photographs in the rows of frames lining the corridors of the school. Her teachers were all from other backgrounds to hers.

Deep down Mia knew she had fought harder for her place in this school. That her grandparents and ancestors fought for this moment. She had travelled further and longer than many of the other students. Her journey even rivalled that of the international boarders.

Mia stood in the corridor between classes, waiting for Naya to come out from the bathroom. Students milled around like river currents. Mia stood by the wall, like she would on the riverbank. She looked at the frames with photographs of previous students, at the award plaques from many different competitions, like she would look at the trees and the hills back home.

'Watch out, loser,' Charlotte said as she pushed by Mia, her shoulder driving into Mia's side. 'Sniffing around by the toilets like a dirty bush rat.'

Mia felt anger rise in her like a flood. Her fists clenched at her sides and her jaw tightened as she stared down Charlotte and her group brushing past in the crowded hall.

Forgetting Tilly's advice, which she had been following for so long, Mia flattened her hands and pushed Charlotte hard on both sides of her shoulders. 'Move over, Charlotte, you don't own the school. And you don't know me.'

Charlotte's mouth opened in surprise, then twisted into a smirk as she stumbled dramatically and tripped to the ground.

'Not a bush rat then, maybe a dumb boxing kangaroo,' Charlotte hissed from the ground,

as her friends rushed over to lift her up. 'You'll regret that. Right girls, my witnesses to this unprovoked attack.'

'Nothing but a basic criminal,' one of Charlotte's friends laughed. 'Knew she didn't belong here.'

Naya came out of the toilets as Charlotte and her group rushed down the hallway towards the principal's office. It didn't take her long to realise something was wrong. Mia quickly filled her in.

Naya's face dropped into a sad frown. 'She doesn't know you, Mia. You are a strong and proud Jaru girl from the Kimberley. You are dirrarn totem. You are deadly. Even if she tricks this mob here, you will always be better than Charlotte.'

Mia felt trapped. Charlotte's web had wrapped around her, making it hard for her to breathe. She wished she could escape, run until she soared above the clouds and arrive back home. She felt that she had let down her mother, her grandparents and all those who believed in her. They'd been the wind under her wings supporting her to come here.

'I reckon you just go there,' Naya said, pointing down the hall. 'Don't let her tell those lies and then have them come hunt you down.'

Mia nodded, fighting back angry tears. Straightening her shoulders and sticking out her chin, she walked beside Naya down the hall, to the principal's office.

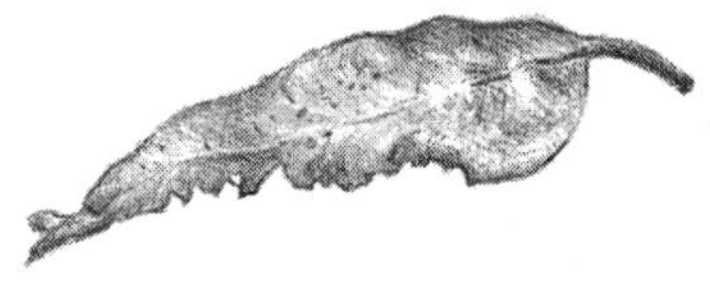

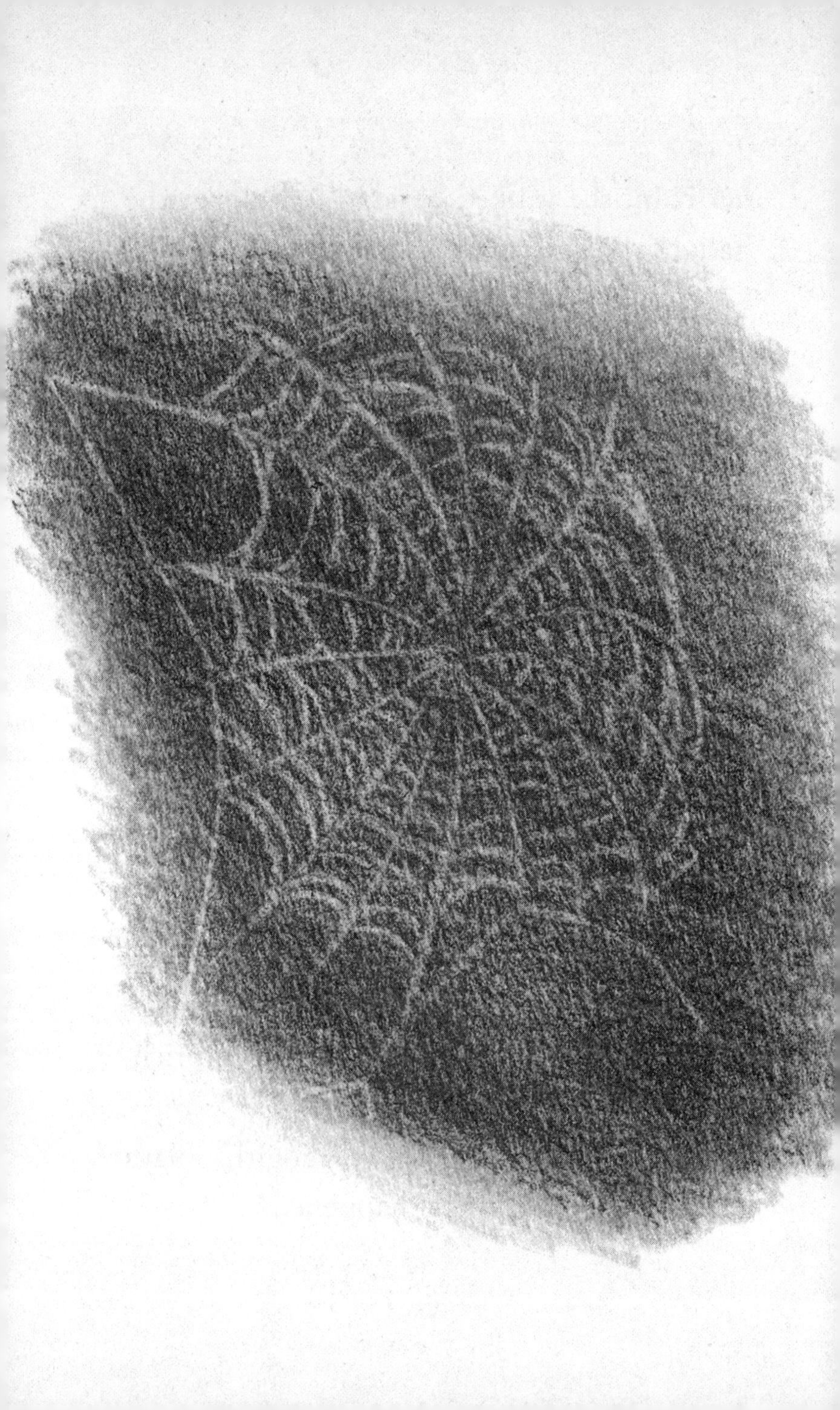

9

The principal's door was closed when Mia arrived. Naya sat on the waiting chair. Mia paced, her tummy was tight at the thought of the lies Charlotte was telling just beyond the door.

'Charlotte won't mention the weeks of bullying, the fact she bumped into me and said horrible things,' Mia whispered to Naya, aware of the other office staff nearby. 'Charlotte probably making me sound like some wild girl out to hurt the innocent, rich, white girls.'

'Stand in your truth, Mia-girl,' Naya replied. 'We know what happened.'

The bell went, but Naya didn't leave Mia's side. Together they waited.

Finally, the principal opened the door and ushered Charlotte and her friends out. She looked surprised to see Naya and Mia waiting outside.

'Please wait there, girls,' she said sternly, brow drawn down in thought as she watched to make sure Charlotte and her gang walked the full length of the hallway before turning back into her office. 'I will call you in soon.'

Mia and Naya were left looking at the closed door. Mia looked out the window at the white cockatoos ripping nuts and fruit off a tall tree, with their strong beaks and claws.

The door cracked open. 'Come in, Mia. Please wait, Naya.'

Mia perched on the edge of the seat on the opposite side of the desk from the principal.

'This is a serious accusation, Mia. With the

prior incident of your physical interactions with Charlotte, this could have very serious consequences,' the principal began. 'But I would like to hear your side of the story.'

Mia sat up straight, and told her side of the story, starting from the beginning – weeks before. She shared how she didn't know if she could prove anything and that it would always be Charlotte's word against hers, and how Charlotte often reminded Mia of her superior place as a high fee-paying student. Mia explained her lack of trust after the first incident. The principal's face remained neutral and open, nodding as Mia told her story.

When Mia had finished, the principal asked her to wait outside while she heard Naya's version. After a short time the principal opened the door again and said, 'Come in, Mia.'

Naya reached for Mia's hand and gave it

a squeeze before resting her hands back in her lap.

'You see those black circles on the roof? They are security cameras,' the principal said, pointing out into the hallway before she shut the door again and walked to her desk. 'I have access to all video feeds on my computer, which I have reviewed. I have heard both of your stories, and heard Charlotte's.'

Mia held her breath.

'The footage around the bathroom is very clear,' the principal said. 'I can see that Charlotte instigated the situation and that she exaggerated her response. The ongoing racism and bullying is not acceptable at our school.'

Mia let out her breath; the principal had believed her.

'We are a hands-off school, Mia,' the principal said sternly. 'So you will need to have consequences. You can trust that Charlotte will be dealt with for her behaviour, too.'

Mia accepted her detention happily, and left the office with Naya walking quickly behind.

'What do you think will happen to Charlotte?' Naya asked as an office staff member walked briskly past them towards their classroom.

'Looks like she might have got caught up in her own web of lies,' Mia said with a smile, as the staff member walked back past them with Charlotte walking behind. 'As long as they keep her away from us.'

10

Mia woke early, so excited for her flight back home and the start of the Easter school holidays that she couldn't sleep. Bleary-eyed, she peaked under the blind into the dim, early dawn light. She picked up her water bottle off the bedside table and shook the limited contents. Thirsty, she walked past her packed bags, the ones that had been packed long before Ms Babel had instructed the students to, and out into the shared corridor. Quietly, she walked into the kitchen and filled up her bottle. As Mia sipped the cool water, she heard Ms Babel and Mr Cale's voices in the common room.

'I'm worried for them,' Mia could hear Ms Babel say. 'Those girls can be anything they want to be. I just worry that some of them might think code-switching, homesickness and this different school are all too much and that they won't come back.'

Mia remembered the times when she had felt just that this term. She knew it was pretty common for kids from her community to try 'schooling away' at boarding school, but then stay in community after the first term. The pull from home was strong. Those students had talked about how hard it had been missing funerals, celebrations, cultural ceremonies, how they missed time out bush with their families. Mia now knew the ache in her chest when she thought of that, too.

'They are just tired,' Mr Cale consoled. 'You and I have seen many students from the outback and even internationally come through here over the years. It's not about how long any of our students stay, it's about what they take away. We've just got to make sure we show these students the possibilities that are out there … and in them. If it's the right path, they will come back.'

'Not all paths are clear,' Ms Babel said. 'I guess I just don't want them getting lost along the way and wishing they had travelled a little longer on this road.'

Mia knew only snippets of Ms Babel's and Mr Cale's lives. Ms Babel's family had lived in Perth for a few generations after migrating from England. She'd told them all stories about the time she'd gone back to England to see where her great-grandparents had come from and meet distant relatives. She felt this gentle pull of recognition in her belly she said, but that place was so cold and different from Noongar Country; where she was born and was lucky enough to call home. Mia felt it hard to relate to what Ms Babel had shared. She couldn't imagine calling any other place home. Interesting how Ms Babel's intergenerational path had brought her here.

Mr Cale was Noongar. Living and working on his Country. Helping First Nations kids to feel comfortable and safe on his land so they could chase their dreams and walk their own paths. He had travelled up through the Goldfields, Pilbara and Kimberley meeting families a few years ago. He'd even travelled overseas to study at a big international university. His path had taken him many places, but always home.

Naya and Mia had already planned what they would do in their own communities: fishing, hunting, going to the pool, road trips, camping out at cousin-sisters' houses. They told each other about the best places around their communities, stories of their funny families. Mia and Naya had also made plans about what they would do when they returned to boarding school. They'd talked excitedly about the classes they were looking forward to now that Charlotte had been 'transferred' to a different school – or so she said. Mia was pretty sure that Naya would return when she did. But she would understand if Naya did not.

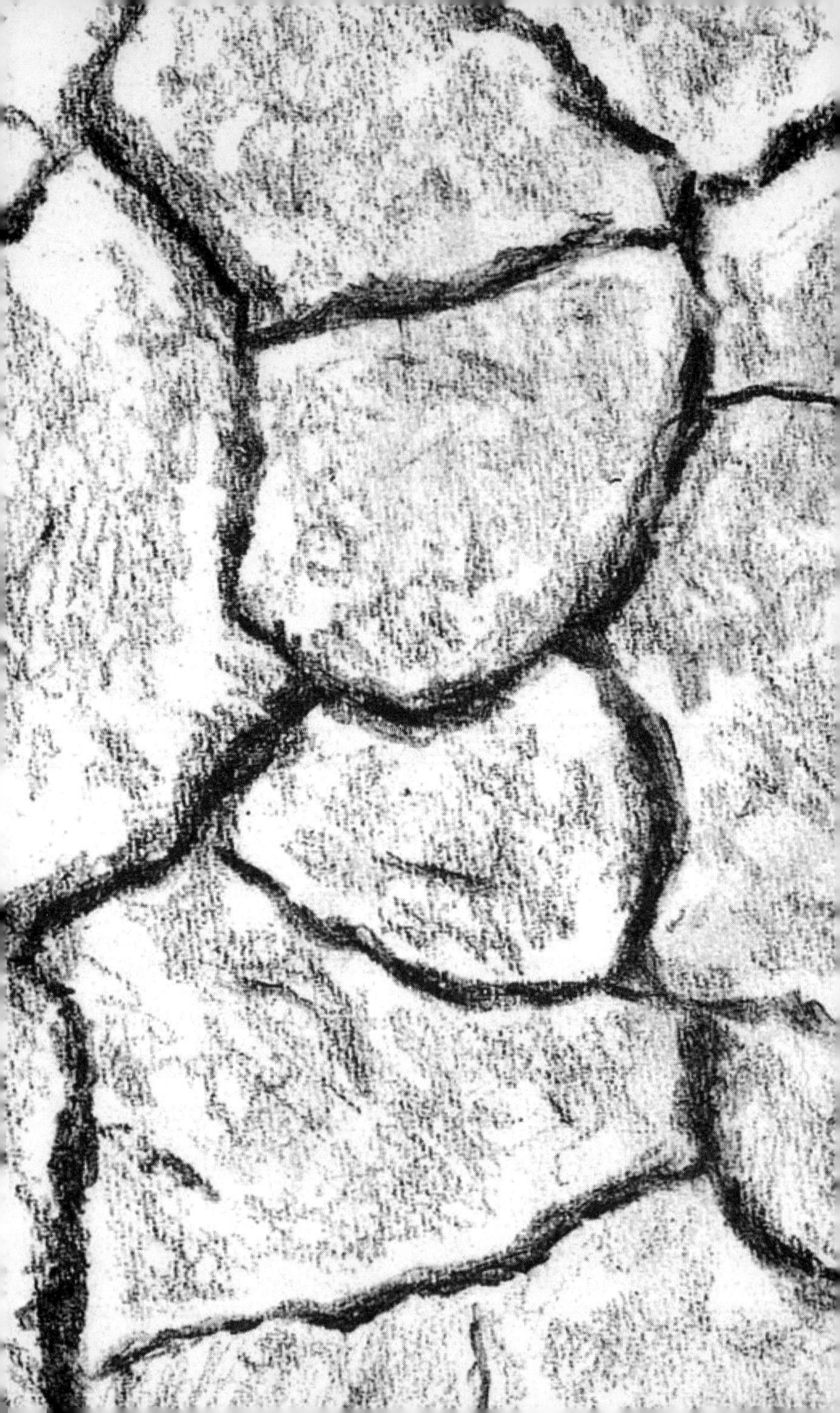

11

The mail plane landed with a thump on the red dirt airstrip. Mia still wasn't used to this flying business. Going to boarding school in January had been her first time on an aeroplane. This was her second and her tummy did backflips on take-off and landing. All this was nothing, because Mia just wanted to jump off the plane and run into her mother's arms. She could see Katherine under the tin shed terminal smiling and waving, Jaja standing nearby, and her cousin-brother Scotty leaning against the chainmail fence.

Finally, they were off and Mia ran into her mother's arms.

Scotty scooped up her bag, 'Good to see you, cuz.'

'What you doing in town, cuz?' Mia asked, falling into place beside him as they walked out of the tiny airstrip boundary. Scotty looked different from when she had last seen him before Christmas, just before they'd taken Jy out bush for ceremony.

'I'm hungry for chocolate, or what?' he laughed, making bunny ears above his head. 'Or maybe I can get me some of that rabbit stew? I don't mind either way!'

Jaja laughed and smiled at her grandson, 'You look like you could use some good fat tucker, too. All muscle working out on the station, hey?'

Jaja was known for her fried damper, called 'fat tucker'. She made a pretty awesome stew as well, but Mia was not sure anyone up here had ever made rabbit stew given that you would be hard-pressed to see one. Rabbits were the feral pests that plagued down south and across the east coast, like wild cats, wild dogs, camels, pigs and donkeys were the ferals of up north.

'Meanwhile, Mia would be full of all that fancy Perth food, na,' Scotty teased playfully. 'Don't worry Jaja, I'll eat her share.'

'Mia probably starving for proper bush food,' Katherine said with a smile. 'Don't worry, we will head down to the river later, catch you some big balga.'

'You can have your bunny stew, cuz,' Mia laughed. 'I'll stick with that barra.'

The airstrip was close to Mia's family's house. Mia enjoyed the hot wind whipping around her ankles, the sound of the gunyarr in yards barking as they walked past, the chatter of her family in Aboriginal English and Jaru language. She felt lighter here, back on Country.

Jawiji sat on the front veranda watching for them down the road.

'Yandani, jawiji,' he walked to the gate to greet her with open arms. 'I'm proud of you.'

Mia knew it wasn't just Country she had missed. She lived for this.

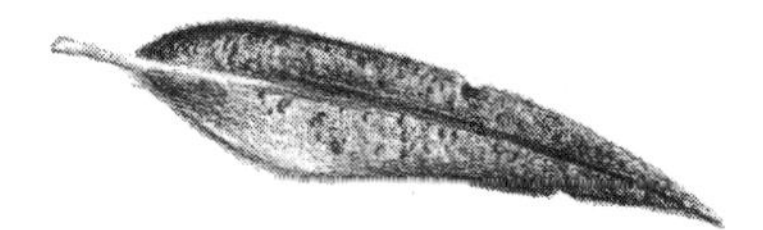

12

'I promised I'd take you,' Scotty said loudly to Mia as they drove along the rough corrugated road out bush. Katherine was in the driver's seat, Jawiji in the front, and Scotty, Jaja and Mia in the back, the boot of the car piled high with bedding and supplies. 'We are close.'

Mia looked over at her grandfather in the passenger seat. This would be an emotional trip for him, too. Last year, Scotty had found a place out on Country with many ancient artifacts from their ancestors. This was where he found the spearhead and had been given permission to give it to Mia. Their Country was so vast, modern history so harsh, that some special places had remained visited by none or few people since invasion and colonisation.

Soon Scotty was pointing off the track into the spinifex bush and beyond. Mia knew that the car could hack it, as it had on hunting trips offroad before, and knew her mother could handle it, too. They took it slower and steadier as they wound their way past anthills, rocks, trees and dips.

Mia's breath caught in her throat as they drove in between two hills showing the cliff face, waterhole and river on the other side. Jy and some other fellas from the station were already there setting up camp. Mia hadn't seen her brother for months and not since he had become a man.

Mia was so happy and ran up to her brother. In her excitement she forgot the tough times they had had just before Christmas and the way Jy had been distant from her, and threw her arms around him in a hug.

'Hey, you know I'm man now,' he smiled and held her back gently. 'You can't run up hugging me anytime now, sis.'

Mia let go and looked at her feet, embarrassed. Culture way, Mia, a girl and his sister, now owed her brother a different kind of respect and should interact with him according to her cultural protocols. Mia was no longer meant to address him by his name. Jy could growl at Mia like an adult now. If Jy wanted to, he could direct her as an adult and she would be expected to listen.

'Glad to see you and have a yarn about your time down Perth,' Jy said. Mia smiled and dodged his repeated attempts to ruffle her hair. 'Might have to come down and sort any boys hanging around.'

Mia laughed, 'Hey, brother, I can sort out my own trouble.'

'I don't doubt it, sis,' Jy said with a smile. 'Go let that serpent know you are here and have a swim to cool down.'

Mia agreed and joined her mother and grandparents by the water as the other men unpacked the supplies from their car. Jaja and Jawiji were standing in silence looking out over the water and cliff face.

‘This is a special place,’ Jawiji said. ‘A gathering place for our mob with this fresh water and bush food around. There are paintings and caves you aren’t allowed to go to, sacred places, over that way.’

‘Been a long time since we have been here,’ Jaja said, scooping down to pick up a rock, rubbing it under her arm and throwing it out into the water. She said her name, Rosa, and her bush name.

‘We should do smoking ceremony,’ Jawiji said, as Katherine and Mia repeated the process that Rosa had done to let the spirits of the living water and this gathering place know they had come.

Mia bent down and scooped the cool fresh water over her face and neck, across her arms and down her legs. She felt the dust of the trip wash away and enjoyed the feeling of the fresh water evaporating the heat from her skin.

Mia helped gather the gum leaves and sticks for the fire and put them in the big old flour drum ready for the Smoking. Nearby the coals in the goongun covered the bin.girrjaru the men had caught earlier. Mia couldn't wait to add some yagu from the waterhole to the bush food later.

Everyone gathered respectfully around the smoking fire when it was ready. Jawiji welcomed everyone back to Country, and told the ancestors they were there. Mia walked through the gentle eucalyptus that cleansed her and protected her on this place. They all did.

Mia felt a heaviness she had been carrying with her since she had gone away drop from her. The homesickness, the culture shock, the isolation, the impact Charlotte had had, the ache for home.

Now her belly just ached for the bin.girrjaru that the older men were now digging out from the sand and coals. And that ache, was easily fixed.

13

It was the afternoon on the last night before Mia was to catch the plane back to boarding school. Sitting with Jaja in the backyard, Mia rested her back against the big tree. Next to this old tree, the dirrarn cage sat empty from when she had freed the rescued bird months ago. Mia remembered the feelings of helplessness about not being able to heal the bird and its sadness as it paced behind the bars. Mia had left the cage door open for the bird and left it to the animal to decide if it would stay or leave.

The dense shade of the old tree and a light breeze provided relief from the heat.

'I don't want to go back,' Mia told her Jaja Rosa. 'I want to stay here.'

Jaja didn't speak for a while, her hands busy, paintbrush dancing over her canvas.

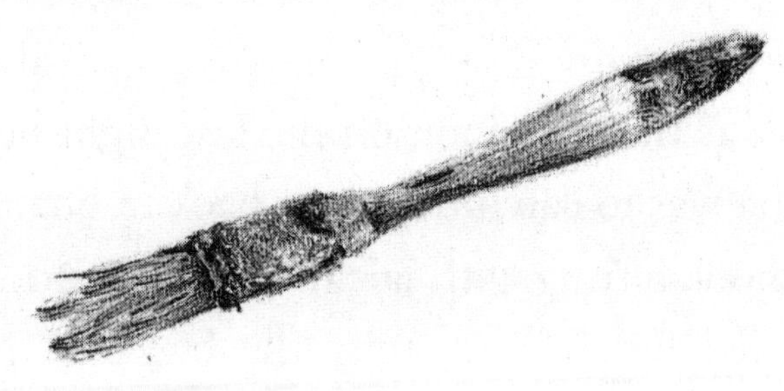

'I thought I could go back,' Mia felt the need to push her point. 'I thought I was getting stronger. But I will miss everyone so much.'

Jaja passed her thc spare brush, silent still. Mia looked at the art on the canvas, the raw earthy colours of the ochre that her grandmother had collected from the special places on Country. These ancient colours, were mixed and spread with modern tools onto modern canvas.

'You remember when you first tried painting?' Jaja said.

Mia shook her head. She couldn't remember the first time. She felt like she had always been sitting down with her grandmother or an aunty this way.

'When you are little you hold the brush wrong. Working with your hands feels better. You can't think of what to draw. You just go with what feels right.'

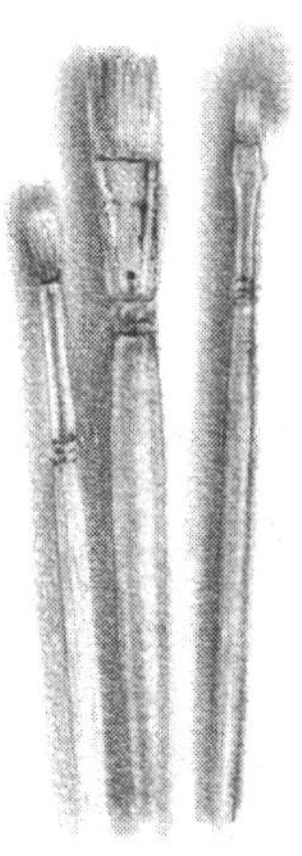

Mia remembered swirling her fingers in sand and dust telling stories by the river, she remembered crushing the ochre with her aunties and feeling the particles getting sticky as they poured just the right amount of water, she remembered making handprints and dots with her fingers on large rocks by waterholes, then later on her grandmother's canvases.

'Then as you get older, you learn to work with your brush and do new strokes,' Jaja continued speaking and painting. 'You might learn from someone new, too. And as you do you can create paintings that are different and capture things you could never see before. Not better – just different.' Mia dipped her brush into the ochre and added her marks to the canvas alongside her Elder.

'Well, this schooling away thing is like that. The first time you go you might feel like you are doing it wrong. You might want to work the way you are used to, speak the way you are used to, you miss the things you usually do. You can't think of anything but our way, our culture, our home. It just doesn't feel right. But as you persist you learn to do things the other way too, to do new things, to live two-way. You are two-ways strong. You can walk in both worlds with confidence. You can create a life wherever you want and capture different things.'

Mia let her grandmother's words float over her and settle in her heart. She was the creator of her own life. She held the brush. She chose the strokes.

'You don't have to go away, my granddaughter,' Jaja said. 'You can be just as strong here on Country. Our children who stay can be anything they want to be. We will teach you things you would never learn in the city whether you stay or go. But that choice is up to you.'

Mia looked around the yard and into the distance beyond her community. This had been her canvas for so many years. It held so many stories – both ancient and new. She thought back to the colours of the animals at the Perth Zoo, to the different colours and patterns as she had flown over Perth, to the new people she had met and the new things she had done on her most recent life canvas.

Mia knew that she could use the skills she had learned in both to paint a bright future – wherever and however she wanted.

A strong wind blew, ruffling the painting between the two. Mia could feel the future calling her. She knew what to do.

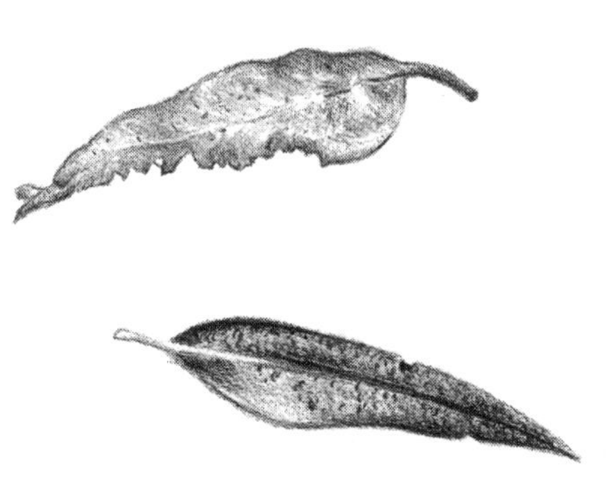

Jaru people are from the East Kimberley (in Western Australia) and their traditional homelands cover approximately 23,591 square kilometres of country.

Glossary of Jaru, Kriol, Aboriginal English (AE) & Noongar words

balga	Jaru	barramundi
bi	AE	slang term meaning 'eh?'
bin.girrjaru	Jaru	bush turkey
booloomun	Kriol	bull/bullock
code-switching		alternating between two or more languages or varieties of language in conversation
cousin-brother	AE	a close male cousin of one's own generation, that is culturally a brother
cousin-sister	AE	a close female cousin of one's own generation, that is culturally a sister
cuz	AE	slang term for cousin
dirrarn	Jaru	black cockatoo; when seen in large numbers, the cockatoos tell locals the, rains are coming

fat tucker	AE	fried damper
gaalyalya	Jaru	white cockatoo
galbun	Jaru	hawk
goongun	Jaru	earth oven, hole
gunyarr	Jaru	dog
jaja	Jaru	grandmother/Grandchild; a respectful term of address used by both members of the pair (see Jawiji), language name shared with other surrounding language groups
jarrambayi	Jaru	goanna, language name shared with other surrounding language groups
jarriny	Jaru	conception totem
jawiji	Jaru	grandfather/grandchild; a respectful term of address used by both members of the pair (see Jaja), language name shared with other surrounding language groups

jiyirr	Jaru	rainbow bee-eater birds
karrak	Noongar	black cockatoo
la	Kriol	preposition meaning *on, in, at* or *to*
marlu	Jaru	kangaroo, language name shared with other surrounding language groups
porcupine	AE	echidna
yagu	Jaru	fish
yandani	Jaru	welcome

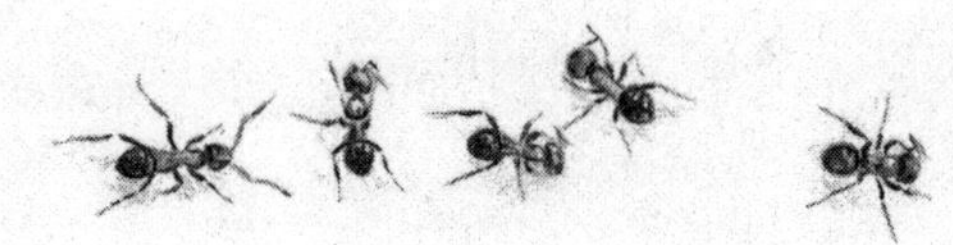

Praise for *Black Cockatoo*

'This deceptively simple tale has a quiet power... It is a reminder that gentleness is a form of strength.'

– Judges comments, *Readings Children's Book Prize*

'A delicate balance is maintained between presenting Indigenous culture in a way which inspires admiration and presenting the challenges faced in communities.'

– Judges comments, *CBCA Book of the Year: Younger Readers*

'This is a highly original and gentle small tale set in the Kimberley about the power of standing up for yourself, your culture and ever-present family ties.'

– Halls Creek Herald

'Subtle and touching, *Black Cockatoo* reaches into the heart and will speak to anyone's need to find their place in this world and the freedom to do so.'

– Writing WA

'Reading *Black Cockatoo*, I am not only proud of these local writers but also so proud to read stories that as a bush community person I can identify with and share with our kids so they can be proud of their lifestyle and their differences.'

– Tammy, *reader review*